Three Questions

*The Wisdom of the Present Moment
and the Power of Compassion*

A Modern Translation

Adapted for the Contemporary Reader

Leo Tolstoy

Translated by Tim Zengerink

Table of Contents

Preface - Message to the Reader

What If You Could Help Rebuild the Greatest Library in Human History?

Thousands of years ago, the Library of Alexandria stood as the crown jewel of human achievement — a sanctuary where the collected wisdom of every known civilization was gathered, preserved, and shared freely.

And then, it was lost.

Through fire, conquest, and the slow erosion of time, humanity lost not just books — but ideas, dreams, discoveries, and stories that could have changed the world forever.

Today, the Library of Alexandria lives again — and you are invited to be a part of its restoration.

Our mission is simple yet profound:

To rebuild the greatest library the world has ever known, and to translate all timeless works into every language and dialect, so that no seeker of knowledge is ever left behind again.

By joining our movement to rebuild the modern Library of Alexandria, you become part of an unprecedented mission:

Unlimited Access to the Greatest Audiobooks & eBooks Ever Written:

Instantly explore thousands of legendary works—Plato, Shakespeare, Jane Austen, Leo Tolstoy, and countless more. All instantly available to read or listen, placing a complete literary universe at your fingertips.

Beautiful Paperback & Deluxe Editions at Printing Cost

Own any title as an elegant paperback, deluxe hardcover, or stunning collectible boxset—offered to you at true printing cost, delivered straight to your door. Build your personal Library of Alexandria, crafted for beauty, built for durability, and worthy of proud display.

Fresh Translations for Modern Readers—in Every Language & Dialect

Enjoy timeless masterpieces reimagined in clear, contemporary language—no more outdated phrases or obscure references. Alongside the original versions, we're tirelessly translating these classics into every language and dialect imaginable, ensuring accessibility and understanding across cultures and generations.

Join a Global Renaissance of Literature & Knowledge

You directly support expanding our library, publishing deluxe editions at true cost, translating works into all global languages, and bringing humanity's greatest stories to people everywhere. By joining today, you're not just preserving a legacy of masterpieces; you set in motion a powerful wave of literary accessibility.

Become a Torchbearer of Knowledge.

Join us for free now at **LibraryofAlexandria.com**

Together, we will ensure that the light of human wisdom never fades again.

With gratitude and a shared love of knowledge,

The Modern Library of Alexandria Team

Visit:

www.libraryofalexandria.com

Or scan the code below:

Introduction

Timeless Answers to Life's Most Urgent Dilemmas

Leo Tolstoy's Three Questions is a literary gem of elegant simplicity and philosophical depth—a parable that contains the distilled wisdom of Tolstoy's mature ethical vision. Written in 1885, during the period following his spiritual transformation, this short story delivers a concise, almost meditative answer to three existential questions that haunt every human being: When is the right time to act? Who is the most important person? And what is the most important thing to do?

These questions form the basis of a tale that unfolds like a moral fable, yet resonates with the power of lived truth. Through the journey of a king who sets out to find definitive answers to these pressing dilemmas, Tolstoy weaves a narrative that challenges the reader to reconsider the way we prioritize time, relationships, and responsibilities. The king consults scholars, mystics, and learned men but finds no satisfying answers. It is only through an encounter with a humble hermit—and a series of seemingly unrelated events—that he comes to realize the truth: the most important time is now; the most important person is the one you are with; and the most important action is to do good to that person.

These conclusions are not presented as doctrinal claims or theological insights, but as self-evident moral truths, revealed through lived experience rather than philosophical argument. And that is where the story finds its enduring power. In an era obsessed with productivity, strategic planning, and self-optimization, Three Questions gently but firmly redirects our attention back to presence, humility, and compassion. In fewer than two thousand words, Tolstoy accomplishes what entire tomes of philosophy struggle to do: he clarifies how to live well.

Practical Philosophy in Parable Form:
A Guide to Moral Clarity

Tolstoy was no stranger to complex moral questions. Having penned masterpieces like War and Peace and Anna Karenina, he turned in his later years to simpler forms of storytelling that allowed him to reach a broader audience with clearer messages. Three Questions stands among his most accessible and universal works. Like the parables of Jesus—whose teachings Tolstoy revered above all others—this story doesn't preach but illustrates. The reader is invited not merely to agree with Tolstoy's answers but to experience their validity through the king's transformation.

The king in the story is not wicked or foolish; he is thoughtful and sincere, a seeker of truth. His questions are not abstract—they arise from the real pressures of ruling wisely and ethically. Yet his search leads him to confusion, because he looks for certainty in systems, in specialists, and in abstract theories. It is only when he leaves the palace—both literally and metaphorically— that clarity comes. The hermit, living simply and quietly, is not interested in pontificating. He responds to the king's presence with action, not advice. And through helping the hermit and saving a wounded stranger, the king receives his answers not from words but from deeds.

This story reflects the core of Tolstoy's moral theology, which had by this time fully rejected institutionalized religion in favor of a radically personal, ethical Christianity. For Tolstoy, the kingdom of God was not found in ritual or dogma, but in action— especially the action of love in the present moment. He believed that truth was not hidden in esoteric texts or academic arguments, but visible in daily life, available to every person regardless of education or status. This belief is what gives Three Questions its extraordinary accessibility: anyone can understand it, and everyone can live it.

The answers offered in the story are deceptively simple. "Now" is always the only moment in which we can act. "The person you are with" is the only one to whom we can show love. And "doing good" is the only thing that can truly fulfill our purpose. These principles apply equally to kings and commoners, to intellectuals and laborers. They demand no theological alignment, only ethical presence. And in this universality lies their enduring relevance.

This modern translation of Three Questions retains the parable's spiritual clarity and narrative grace while updating its language to resonate with contemporary readers. It has been rendered with particular attention to preserving the calm, reflective tone of Tolstoy's original, and to highlighting the simple beauty of the story's structure and message.

In conclusion, Three Questions is not only a story—it is a compass. It invites readers to pause in a world of relentless motion and to rediscover what truly matters. It does not require study or interpretation, only attention. And in giving that attention, one may find not just the answer to the king's questions, but to one's own. For in the moment we awaken to the truth of presence, compassion, and purposeful action, we no longer need to ask when, who, or what. We already know. And we are ready to live.

Three Questions

One day, a king had a thought: if he always knew the best time to start something, the right people to listen to and avoid, and the most important thing to focus on, he would never fail in anything he tried to do.

Wanting to find these answers, he announced across his kingdom that he would reward anyone who could teach him the perfect time for every action, the most important people to pay attention to, and how to know what truly mattered most.

Many wise men came to the king, but they all gave different answers.

For the first question, some said the only way to know the right time for everything was to create a strict schedule, planning out days, months, and years in advance. By following this schedule, everything would be done at the perfect time. Others argued that planning ahead was useless because the right time for something could not be decided in advance. Instead, they said the king should always be alert, pay attention to everything happening around him, and act when the moment was right. Another group believed that no single person, not even a king, could always make the right decision alone. They suggested that he form a council of wise advisors who would help him decide the best time for every action.

But then others disagreed, saying that some decisions had to be made immediately and could not wait for a council's advice. In those cases, the only way to know what to do was to predict the future. Since only fortune tellers and magicians could do that, they claimed the king should rely on them to find the right timing for everything.

The answers to the second question were just as different. Some said the most important people for the king were his advisors, while others believed they were priests. Some argued that doctors were the most necessary, while others insisted that warriors mattered most.

The third question, about what the most important work was, also had many answers. Some said science was the most valuable thing in the world. Others believed military skill was most important, while another group argued that religious devotion mattered more than anything else.

Since everyone gave different answers, the king could not decide which was correct. He refused to reward anyone, but he still wanted to find the truth. So, he decided to seek the advice of a wise hermit, who was known across the land for his wisdom.

The hermit lived deep in a forest and never left his home. He also only spoke to ordinary people, never to rulers or nobles. So, the king dressed in simple clothes, left his guards behind, and rode toward the hermit's home. Before he reached the hermit's small hut, he got off his horse and walked the rest of the way alone.

As the king approached, he saw the hermit digging the ground in front of his small hut. The hermit, who looked old and weak, greeted the king but kept working. With each movement of his spade, he struggled to catch his breath.

The king moved closer and said, "Wise hermit, I have three questions for you. How can I know the right time to do something? Who are the most important people in my life, the ones I should focus on the most? And what things should always be my top priority?"

The hermit heard him but didn't answer. Instead, he wiped his hands, spat on them for a better grip, and kept digging.

"You seem tired," the king said. "Let me help you with that."

The hermit nodded and handed over the spade. "Thank you," he said, sitting down on the ground.

The king worked for a while, digging two rows of soil. Then he stopped and repeated his questions. Again, the hermit gave no reply. Instead, he stood up, reached for the spade, and said, "Now, rest for a bit and let me do some work."

But the king did not give back the spade. He kept digging. An hour passed, then another. The sun was beginning to set behind the trees when the king finally put the spade down.

"I came to you for answers," he said. "If you cannot give them to me, just say so, and I will return home."

The hermit glanced up. "Someone is running toward us," he said. "Let's see who it is."

The king turned and saw a bearded man emerging from the woods, clutching his stomach. Blood seeped between his fingers as he staggered forward. As soon as he reached the king, he collapsed to the ground, moaning weakly.

The king and the hermit rushed to help him. They loosened his clothing and found a deep wound in his stomach. The king washed the wound as best he could and used his own handkerchief, along with a towel from the hermit, to bandage it. But the bleeding wouldn't stop. Again and again, the king replaced the blood-soaked cloth, cleaned the wound, and carefully wrapped it again. Finally, the bleeding slowed, and the man regained consciousness.

He whispered for water. The king quickly brought him fresh water and helped him drink. By then, the sun had set, and the air had cooled. With the hermit's help, the king carried the wounded man into the hut and laid him on the bed.

The man soon closed his eyes and fell asleep. The king, worn out from walking, digging, and taking care of him, sat down by the door. Before long, he also drifted off into a deep sleep and didn't wake up until the next morning.

When he opened his eyes, it took him a moment to remember where he was. He looked over at the bed and saw the bearded man watching him with a serious expression.

"Please forgive me," the man said in a weak voice.

The king looked at him, confused. "I don't know you," he replied. "I have no reason to forgive you."

"You don't know me, but I know you. I was once your enemy—the man who swore to get revenge

14

because you had my brother executed and took his land. When I found out you were traveling alone to see the hermit, I planned to ambush you on your way back. But as the day passed and you didn't return, I left my hiding place to look for you. That's when I ran into your guards. They recognized me right away and attacked, leaving me badly wounded. I barely managed to escape, but I would have died from my injuries if you hadn't helped me.

I wanted to take your life, but instead, you saved mine. Now, if I survive and if you allow it, I will serve you loyally, and I will tell my sons to do the same. Please forgive me!"

The king was happy to have settled things so easily with his enemy and to have gained a new friend instead. He not only forgave the man but also promised to send his personal doctor and servants to take care of him. He even said he would return his land.

After saying goodbye to the wounded man, the king stepped onto the porch and looked around for the hermit. Before leaving, he wanted to ask his questions one last time. He spotted the hermit outside, kneeling in the garden, planting seeds in the soil they had dug the day before.

The king walked over and said, "Please, wise man, answer my questions just once more."

The hermit, still crouched on the ground, looked up at the king and said, "But you have already been given your answers!"

The king was confused. "What do you mean? How have my questions been answered?"

The hermit said, "Think about it. If you hadn't stopped to help me yesterday by digging those garden beds, you would have left, and that man would have attacked you. Then you would have wished you had stayed. So at that moment, the most important time was when you were digging, and I was the most important person. The best thing you could do then was to help me.

"Later, when the wounded man came running toward us, the most important time was when you cared for him. If you hadn't helped, he would have died without making peace with you. So at that moment, he was the most important person, and saving his life was the most important thing you could do.

"Remember this: the most important time is always right now because it's the only moment we can control. The most important person is the one you are with because no one knows what will happen in the future. And the most important thing to do is to help others because that is why we are here."

Thank You for Reading

Dear Reader,

We hope this timeless classic has sparked your imagination and enriched your literary journey. Now that you've turned the final page, we want to share a vision for the future of reading—one where every classic you've ever wanted to explore is at your fingertips, in a format that best suits your life.

We'd like to invite you to gain immediate, unlimited digital & audiobook access to hundreds of the most treasured literary classics ever written—along with the option to secure deluxe paperback, hardcover & box set editions at printing cost. Together, we can spark a new global literary renaissance alongside our small, independent publishing house called "The Library of Alexandria."

Thousands of years ago, the Library of Alexandria stood as a beacon of knowledge—until it was lost to history. We aim to reignite that spirit of preservation and discovery right now, in the modern age—only this time, it's accessible to all, in every language and every format.

Picture a world where every timeless classic, novel, poem, or philosophical treatise is not only available to read but also updated for today's readers—modernized, translated into any language or dialect, and ready to enjoy in any format you choose, whether that is in an eBook, audiobook, paperback, or deluxe hardcover & box set version a printing cost.

By joining our movement to rebuild the modern Library of Alexandria, you become part of an unprecedented mission to offer:

Unlimited Audiobook & eBook Access to the Greatest Classics of All Time

Instantly explore thousands of legendary works, from Plato and Shakespeare to Jane Austen and Leo Tolstoy. All are instantly ready to read or listen to, giving you a complete literary universe at your fingertips.

Paperback & Deluxe Editions at Printing Costs:

Purchase any title in a paperback, deluxe hardbound, or deluxe boxset edition at printing costs, shipped right to your doorstep. Curate your personal library of Alexandria with editions worthy of display— crafted to last, designed to captivate, and delivered straight to your door.

Modern translations for Contemporary Readers in all languages and dialects

Discover a vast selection of classics reimagined in clear, current language—no more struggling with outdated phrases or obscure references. Next to the original versions, we aim to offer translations in as many languages and dialects as possible.

As we continue our translation efforts and add new languages, readers everywhere can connect with these works as if they were written today. By bridging linguistic divides, you're contributing to ensuring that these timeless stories become more meaningful, accessible, and inspiring for people across the globe.

Your Personal Library of Alexandria:

Over the months and years, you'll curate a unique physical archive of classics—each volume a testament to your taste, curiosity, and love of knowledge. It's not just about owning books—it's about curating a cultural legacy you'll cherish and pass down for generations to come.

Join a Global Literary Renaissance:

Your support fuels an ongoing mission: allowing us to reinvest in offering deluxe print editions (including special boxsets) at their true cost, broaden the range of available formats and translations, and extend the reach of these works to new audiences worldwide. By joining today, you're not just preserving a legacy of masterpieces; you set in motion a powerful wave of literary accessibility.

We are more than a publisher—we're a movement, and we can't do it alone. Your support lets us scale our mission, preserving and reimagining history's greatest works for tomorrow's readers.

Become a Torchbearer of knowledge.

Thank you for picking up this book and allowing us into your literary journey. As you turn the pages, know that you're part of something larger: a global effort to keep these stories alive, share their wisdom across borders and generations, and spark a true cultural revival for the modern era.

If this resonates with you—please consider taking the next step by visiting:

www.libraryofalexandria.com

With gratitude and a shared love of knowledge,

The Modern Library of Alexandria Team

Visit:

www.libraryofalexandria.com

Or scan the code below: